FORGOTTEN SPACES

DhineshSunder Ganapathi

Kindle Direct Publishing

For any queries on the content, reach out to the author at dhineshsunder93@gmail.com

CONTENTS

Title Page

Copyright

Preface

Prologue

THE EMPTINESS

TEAM MEETING

COMMUNICATION   19

COLLABORATION   31

LEADERSHIP   45

POSTMORTEM   55

EPILOGUE   59

To be continued...   61

Acknowledgement   63

About The Author   65

PREFACE

Pandemic has hit us hard, but we are stronger than that, Vaccination is done in a rapid pace across the globe. Multiple variants of covid19 has been found, the fight is not over yet, we are going to win this no matter what, At the time of writting this, offices and schools are opening up, partially. I wish everyone a meticulous courage to be embedded on them to over the come these uncertain times, May the force be with you

◆ ◆ ◆

PROLOGUE

Two days into the lockdown, Pandemic was announced My team was discussing, what is a pandemic, and its impact. We assumed that work from home would last only for 30 days, which gave a hope that things would be back to normal in few weeks, everyone shoot out in joy for the Work from home. I was wondering "when we go back to office. t what about the forgotten spaces, where our things, plants, pedestals lying all open" is it ready to be ghosted!?

THE EMPTINESS

An eerie, almost dreadful feeling clinches your chest when you first enter an empty office. It's a feeling of anticipation that never develops, leaving your soul disappointed and confused by the moment.

As I walk up and down the aisles of empty cubicles, I can almost remember what it was once like. Only a few years ago, this office was bustling with life. When I stand by my corner office door, within the silence, I can almost hear the ringing of phones, the electricity of office chatter, the life that the employees of my company once brought to this space. Now, I'm lucky to hear the ding from the elevator accidentally stopping on the seventh floor.

Honestly, I'm not sure why I bother to keep an office space anymore. Other than the building's owner offering me a deal for the rent, there's no need to continue to pay for a five-thousand square foot office space. Maybe it's a piece of me that pines for the time when we, as in my staff and I, came together to build an empire. Now, that no longer seems possible.

The smartwatch around my left wrist buzzed, reminding me of my meeting at three. Typically, I would schedule my appointments early in the morning, using the excuse that I need to jet off somewhere for lunch. But, who does lunch anymore? At least, I know that if our meetings are scheduled for three that my staff hasn't already snuck off or are making themselves comfortable in their sweat clothes.

One last scan of the room, I notice a computer flickering in the corner near the windows. I take a glance at my watch; I still have five minutes until my staff meeting.

From somewhere in the room, I hear the tapping of fingers on a keyboard. For a moment, I didn't think anything of it. Then I remembered that I was supposed to be the only person in the office.

"Hello? Is anyone here?"

No one responded. In a way, I was hoping to hear someone's voice, even if it was a person from the cleaning crew. Anymore, I seldom listen to a voice that doesn't come from a speaker on my laptop or phone.

A high-pitched beep pierced the silence. I turned, searching for where the sound originated. Another beep sent me spinning on my heels to the left in search of its source. Another beep forced me to look to my right.

"Hey, come on now. It isn't funny. Who's in here?" I demanded to know. This time convinced someone was in the room with me.

A high-pitched buzz came from above me, and I nearly peed my pants. Then I realized that maintenance was probably testing the fire alarms in the building. I laughed and continued to chuckle over my foolishness back to my office.

At the door of my office, I paused and scanned the room again.

"Jessie," a woman's voice called from the empty room.

This time I knew I heard someone call my name.

"Who's there?" I called out.

"We miss you, Jessie."

I took a step back into the cubicles, looking around the dimly lit room for signs of who spoke.

"Who are you? Where are you?" I called back. Only silence returned. "Answer me!"

I remained, scanning the room for anything that moved. For two minutes, I waited, but the woman never revealed herself.

"Fine. If you don't want to show yourself, then see yourself out. It is a private office."

TEAM MEETING

By the time I sat at my desk, it was 3:04. Only Samantha, my Head of Finance, was on the screen. Samantha was what you would expect someone in accounting to look like. She had a skeleton-thin figure that caused me to wonder if she ever ate. Her hair was short and muddy-brown. She also wore glasses with the lens so thick I couldn't tell what her eye colour was. She always wore the same three sweaters, even during the summer months. All that matter to me was that she was consistent and excellent at her job.

Next on the line was my head of production, Bob Mayor. Bob was the complete opposite of Samantha when it came to his weight. Three hours passed for lunch, and he still had a sub sandwich in his hand. I've nearly fired him so many times; I'm not sure why he's still working for me. However, for the time being, he would be impossible to replace.

My Head of Marketing, Margo, popped on the screen. Margo was one of those overly creative people who changed jobs as quickly as her nail polish. She was another one of my staff heads that made me wonder why I hadn't fired her yet. Yet, somehow she brought the company a staggering number of clients last year. Instead of firing her, as I intended, I gave her a raise and a large bonus.

Last on the screen was Rick. He was the head of Logistics. By the far-off look in his eyes, I doubted he had anything to report. I kept him on because he knew how to get the job done.

"Hi everyone. How's everybody's day going so far?" Margo began in a sing-song pop voice that made me believe she would be far better in a music career, not selling canned fruits and vegetables.

The four continued on talking about their week, mainly about personal matters; Samantha's three cats, Bob's lost lunch order, Margo's new boyfriend... and Rick; well, Rick didn't have much to say at all. Rick sat staring at the computer like he wasn't even present.

It was then I realized we were missing one person, my head of Research and Development.

"Anyone knows where Mike Matten's at today?" I asked.

Margo shook her head. "I heard he had a family emergency. Maybe Linda in HR would know more?" she said.

I agreed. "I'll give her a call after this and see what she knows."

"Hey, Rick, how's your week treating you so far?" I asked, quieting the others from their non-employment discussion.

Rick nodded but didn't say anything.

"You don't look well. Are you doing okay?" I asked with concern. Even when I hired Rick, he looked like he was on drugs. This time though, something seemed off by his strange expression.

Rick slowly nodded. "Yes."

I didn't believe him. Rick was usually the person in the group that had a joke to start every meeting. Most of the time, Rick's jokes weren't appropriate, but no one complained. This time, no, something was different with Rick.

Bob started the meeting about our current production times, speaking as he continued to scarf down his foot-long hoagie. Then it was Margo's turn. Most of her discussion was about conventions. She and her team had planned to attend several events this year.

Unfortunately, all events were cancelled due to the pandemic. I know this bothered her greatly. She loved attending conventions and spending exorbitant amounts of the company's money on room service. Who knows what else she did during her downtime, and I don't want to know.

Samantha was next on the list. With her, I seldom paid much attention to the numbers unless she reported losses. Thankfully, everyone had a desire to stock their shelves during the pandemic. If anything, we couldn't produce enough merchandise.

My eyes gravitated to Rick on my screen. He kept nervously looking over his shoulder. It wasn't the type of look that he was acknowledging someone entering the room. No, this was the kind of look that someone was in the room with him that he didn't want to be.

I typed in the chat box to the right of the screen:

Jessie: Rick – are you sure everything is okay?

Rick's eyes turned to the chatbox, but he remained sternly facing the screen.

Rick: 2247 - Tucson, AZ

Code 2247 referred to lost, stolen, or contaminated merchandise.

By now, the conversation between the others had turned back to their personal lives. Margo had fallen in love with someone who delivered her dinner last night. Again, not appropriate. I longed for the days when office gossip was designated solely to the break room and water cooler.

I ignored their conversation, reading Rick's response over and over. What did he mean by "Tucson, AZ"? Three years ago, we had a warehouse there that burned down in an electrical fire. The company lost five million dollars in products from that incident.

"So... Rick, do you have anything to add to this

conversation?" I spoke up, again interrupting the discussion about whether it's a good idea to get matching tattoos after knowing someone for four hours. Maybe email is better?

"Nothing new to report, Boss. Shi—" A loud chirp interrupted Rick's voice. He glanced over his shoulder, then cleared his throat uneasily. "...Uh, shipping out of Japan is still slow. We don't expect our next shipment of clams for another two weeks, and..." he paused again, tugging at his dress shirt's collar.

"You know we work from home. You don't have to wear dress shirts for video conferencing," Margo spoke up.

"I don't see why not. I'm still paying you to do your jobs. It's good to see one of my employees showing initiative," I pointed out.

A message popped up in the chatbox.

: We miss you.

Samantha blinked several times as she read the message. "Who forgot to add their name?"

Margo: Not me

"Not me," Margo followed.

Bob and Samantha also typed a "here" message.

: When will you return? We're lonely here without you.

"Who's writing that?" I asked. Bob, Samantha, and

Margo all shook their heads.

Rick: 2247

"Okay, if we're all accounted for. Then who's that? Is that Mike?" Margo asked.

"Jessie?" Bob questioned.

I shook my head. "There shouldn't be anyone else in this chat room." A loud clamoring from the other room caused me to raise my hand. "Hold on a second."

COMMUNICATION

I stepped away from my desk and peered out into the office. Clouds overhead caused the room to look darker than the area should have.

"Anyone out here? Speak up, or I'll call security," I demanded, all the while I searched the area around me for anything I could use for a weapon. Something didn't feel right to me.

Three cubicles away, I spotted the baseball bat Juan Salvador kept in his cubical. He was a huge baseball fan and would often head to the field right after work. I received his notice three months prior, yet he hadn't bothered to return to the office to collect his belongings.

Though, it was odd that out of a staff of fifty employees, only six bothered to return to the office to gather their personal items.

I listened, waiting for a response. Nothing heard.

"Hey, Boss!" Bob called out, causing my heart to leap into my throat. I spun around, the bat ready to swing at anything that might be behind me. When I realized it was only Bob, I could feel my cold breath exhale slowly from my lips.

"Yeah," I called back.

"Everything okay?" he asked.

My head bobbed on my shoulders up until I sat down again. "Hold on," I told the group as I dialed down to the security station on the first floor. "Yes, this is Jessie Greenfield on the seventh floor. Could you send someone up here to do a sweep of the area?"

"Hello, Ma'am. Anything, in particular, going on?" asked the security officer.

"I hear a woman's voice, but I couldn't find her. I wanted to make sure she's no longer in the office."

"I'll send someone up," security assured.

I turned my attention back to my team, noticing first their concerned expressions. Then I noticed that Rick's screen was dark. Well, not exactly dark. More like someone had turned off the lights in the room that he was in. What was even stranger was that Rick had left.

"When did Rick leave?" I asked.

The other three turned their attention to the left corner where Rick's image was supposed to be.

"I'm not sure," Bob said.

"We were too busy trying to listen to what was going on in the office with you," Samantha admitted. "Is everything okay there?"

I waved her on, not wanting to focus on what was happening in the office. I was certain security would find whoever was in the office and take care of it for me. What I did want to know was where Rick had disappeared and why he was acting so peculiar.

Bob immediately called Rick's cell phone, then held his phone to the screen so we could hear his voice mail message.

"Why would he leave his screen on?" Samantha mentioned.

I peered through the darkroom, trying to see anything that might give me a clue to where he went. All I could see was a Scindapsus vine hanging along the back of his room. I never pictured Rick as the type of person to own a plant.

"Leave him be, for now. I'll touch base with him later," I decided.

Bob, Margo, and Samantha's eyes all grew wide as if they were watching something behind me.

"What?" I turned to my opaque front wall that faced inside the office to see a dark shadow creep by. Instantly, my hand reached for the baseball bat. I leaned against my desk.

"Boss, I'm coming in. I'll be there in five minutes. Don't leave your office," Bob insisted. He disappeared from the chat before I could tell him not to.

"I'm coming to," Samantha started.

"And do what? At least Bob has muscles," Margo pointed out.

"No, stay on the line in case one of you needs to call the police," I whispered. I didn't realize how frightened I was until I attempted to speak.

I raised the baseball bat to my shoulder and slowly opened my office door.

"Hello?" I called out.

"Ms Greenfield?"

I swung the bat out of fright. Thankfully, Doug, the security guard, had great reflexes and jumped out of the way before I could hit him.

"Whoa now. It's just me," he assured.

My hand flew to my beating chest as my blood rushed to

my head. "Uh, sorry about that. It's a tad spooky with no one around. Did you find who-ever was up here?"

Doug waved for me to follow him down one of the aisles of cubicles. He pointed to a desk. Somehow, the vine plant the employee had left behind had grown around the phone receiver on her desk and knocked it off the base.

"This is the only thing I could find that was making any noise. After a while, if a phone is off the hook for too long, the tone turned to one loud chirp," Doug explained as he hung the phone back. The plant immediately knocked the receiver off the base again. At that point, Doug decided to remove a piece of the plant that was causing problems with his utility knife. He tossed the piece of the plant into the garbage.

"That should be the end of your trespasser," Doug joked. I wasn't convinced. "No, this person specifically called out my name. Could you look around the office one more time? It would rest my mind at ease," I asked. I could still feel my heart beating hard in my chest.

He nodded, grinning as if I were crazy. "Sure."

"I'll be in my office. Swing by when you're sure no one is in here," I said, motioning back to my office.

I was five steps from my office when I heard a loud bang echo from the windows on the other side of the office.

"Doug?" I called out.

A loud, unholy screech cried out, followed by another thump and the sound of a metal desk creaking as if it were being crushed. If I had more sense, I would have run directly into my office, locked the door, and called the police. Instead, I ran towards the noise like the fool I am.

I searched the darkness, wishing I would have turned on the lights. I never think about turning on the lights anymore.

"Doug?" I called hoarsely, panic swelling around my throat.

Against the front windows, I noticed one of the desks had collapsed in the middle as if someone had taken a sludge hammer to the top. I reached for my phone in my pocket, realizing I had left it on my desk.

"Boss!"

COLLABORATION

I swung around with the bat; this time; Bob grabbed the bat. He was standing behind me, panting for breath through his black face mask.

"Nice... swing," he coughed. "I came as quickly as I could."

I had forgotten how large Bob was. He stood six-foot-seven on top of having amble room in his mid-section.

He moved me aside, examining the desk.

"What the hell happened here?" he asked as he rose his cell phone's flashlight to the desk.

"Doug went to check out a noise. The next thing I heard was this," I mentioned.

Bob grew closer, pointing to a trail of blood on the desk.

The trail continued down the aisle then disappeared. He turned his light to the ceiling near the window, motioning to the same plant that had knocked the phone receiver off the base. He followed the plant across the ceiling, revealing that it had grown up into the ceiling joists.

We continued to follow the vines until we came to the area where the blood had disappeared. There was a large bundle of vines all gathered at that point against the ceiling.

The vines opened up, dropping down the skeletal remains of Doug.

At that moment, all I remembered was staring at Bob. It wasn't until we were in my office did I realize that Bob had carried me back to safety.

"Remind me to give you a raise if we make it out alive," I panted for breath. I'm not sure why I was panting. I wasn't the one running with my boss over my shoulder.

Bob sat on the floor next to me, nodding. "What... what was that?"

"Was what? What's going on?" Margo called out from the computer.

"Hey, Jessie. Will this take much more time? My cats are getting hungry and –" Samantha spoke up.

"Pay attention! Something's going on at the office. Jessie? You guys okay?" Margo called out.

I held my hand up to signal we were safe. Well, safe for the moment. I cupped Bob's arm, making sure he was alright. He nodded, still breathing heavily through his mask.

"Who—" I started, being interrupted by a coughing fit. "...what department works by the left corner windows?" I asked. I should have known, but I couldn't recall.

"Research and development," Samantha answered.

"Mike Matten, right. Samantha, get him on the phone for me," I ordered.

"I don't have his—"

"I'll do it. We dated for a microsecond three years ago," Margo mentioned.

"You weren't working for us three years ago," Samantha pointed out.

"How do you think I got this job?" Margo said.

"CALL HIM!" I interrupted.

Then something occurred to me... the plant. I managed to crawl back into my office chair and look at Rick's dark screen. Within his room, I could make out something slithering past the screen, much like a snake. A leaf popped by the screen and then another, followed by... a severed arm. I jumped back, nearly falling out of my chair.

Bob stood beside me, pointing to the screen. "I guess you'll be needing a new logistics manager," he said. By his paling skin and shocked expression, I knew he didn't mean exactly what he said.

My eyes managed to shift away from Rick's screen over to Samantha's. Behind her right shoulder, I noticed the same exact plant sitting on a shelf on the wall. She was too busy petting an orange-striped cat to notice Rick's screen.

"Samantha, who gave you that plant?" I asked calmly.

Samantha looked back at the plant. "Oh, um... Mike gave us all a piece the day before the lockdown. I usually kill plants, but this one has been growing wonderfully. He was using it to test some new fertilizer that was supposed to help produce more fruit."

"Get out of the room," I returned calmly.

"But..."

"Get your cats and get out of that room," I insisted, never raising my voice.

"Okay," she said, stunned. "Dinner time. Go on," she shooed the cat off her lap and carried her laptop into the hallway.

"I can't reach Mike," Margo said in a huff.

"Margo, do you have any plants in your house?" I asked.

Margo shook her head. "Me? Plants? No way. Mike tried to give me one of his, but I gave it to Rick."

Bob's hands shook as he pointed to Samantha's screen. She was standing in the hallway with her laptop.

"What's this all about, Jessie?" she asked. As she spoke, a large piece of the vine grabbed her by the foot. Her laptop crashed to the floor — her screen disappeared.

A message popped up in the chat box: We miss you, Jessie.

I turned to Bob, unsure what to do. "We need to call the police," Bob said in an overly calm voice, yet his eyes were distant.

I broke free of my moment of mental numbness. "What would I tell the police? We're being held captive by a house plant that my head of research developed to take over the world? Should I add that two of my employees and a security guard have been murdered by the same house plant? They'll think we're crazy."

"Well... we have to do something," he

pointed out.

Margo stared at the screen with a mortified expression. "Bleach," she muttered.

"What was that?" I asked.

"You need to kill the plant. There's bleach in the break room. Pour it into the soil, and it should kill the plant almost instantly," she explained.

Bob glanced at me from the corner of his eye. "Almost?"

"We have to try..." I paused, glancing at Bob. As much as I appreciated his help, this was my company. "I have to try," I corrected myself.

"Jessie —" he started to protest.

I shook my head, adamant about my task. "I can't have you risk your life. What would HR say?" I attempted to joke, but jokes weren't my strong suit. That is ... it was Rick's department.

I grabbed the baseball bat and ready myself to open the door. "Stay inside and lock the door behind me. If you hear me give you the code 2247, open the door."

"2247? But, doesn't that mean—"

"It's what Rick was trying to tell me. Lost, stolen, or contaminated. He was trying to warn me that there was a contaminated plant in our office," I explained, now finally understanding what Rick meant. Not that I would have believed him if he told me outright. Who would believe that a houseplant hyped-up on fertilizer would go around killing people?

Bob held my shoulder back before I opened the door. "Stay safe," he warned, then handed me my cell phone.

I nodded but found his words humorous. How could I stay safe with a man-eating plant waiting outside my door? All I could hope for was that I manage to keep two of my limbs.

LEADERSHIP

I stepped outside my office, listening to the door lock behind me. I pointed my phone's flashlight to the ceiling. The plant had now grown through the suspended T-bar ceiling. There was no doubt in my mind that it was only a matter of time before the plant would take over the entire building.

"Hello, Jessie. We've been waiting for you to return. We've been lonely without you," a harmony of voices whispered from around the office.

I started to speak, finding it difficult to form words. "If you miss us, why are you trying to murder us?"

"Murder? No murder. We love you," the plant hissed back.

I tried not to think of my conversation and focused on reaching the break room. The break room was across all four aisles and on the other side of the office. On a typical day, I enjoyed that the break room was so far away from my office. It gave me a chance to stretch my legs. Now, though, I was seriously thinking of having it moved into the empty office near mine.

I crept through the aisle of cubicles. Above me, I could hear the leaves move as if each of the leaves held tiny eyes all watching me.

"Isn't that how you show love, Jessie?

To consume is to show you care," the voices around me continued.

"To consume?" I thought, but I wasn't about to ask. I didn't want any more demonstrations, especially on myself.

I felt a tapping on my shoulder. I turned to find a vine that had wrapped around my baseball bat and coiled down to my shoulder. The bat flew from my grasp, smashing against my office door.

"Boss!" Bob called out behind the door.

"Stay inside," I yelled back.

Weaponless, I ran as fast as I could to the break room. Something grabbed my ankle, and I went flying to the floor. My head smacked the hard ground, and for a few seconds, my eyesight went dark. Then, one inch at a time, I felt my body being dragged back towards the direction of the window. Suddenly, I broke free.

"RUN!" Bob yelled.

I flipped over in time to see Bob, fire axe in hand, swinging at the vine with mad intensity.

"Go! Go! Go!" he yelled, pointing the axe to the break room. He helped me to my feet, and we hurried into the break room.

The door slammed shut behind us as we skidded to the floor near the microwave.

I turned to Bob, gasping for breath. "I thought I told you to stay in my office?" I reprimanded.

"I've never been good with following orders. You know that," he joked.

He crawled to the sink and opened the cabinet door. From inside the cabinet, he removed a gallon of bleach, then crawled back to my side.

"Why do you think he did it?" Bob asked.

"Who did what?"

"Mike? Why did he create a fertilizer that would make a plant grow huge and try to kill us all? I remember he attempted to give everyone in the office a cutting before we went into lockdown. Seems rather convenient that the plant that's killing everyone is the same plant he was handing out around the office."

"Until we know more, we have to give him the benefit of the doubt. We've been meeting online for the past year, and never once did he give me the impression that he was trying to sabotage the company or kill his co-workers," I pointed out. However, Bob did have a valid point.

Bob ignored my comment. He looked like he already had his mind made up. He held up the gallon of bleach. "Now what?"

"We find where this SOB's soil is and take it down," I grumbled. "And I think I know exactly where it is."

Bob handed me the bottle of bleach, picked up his axe then motioned for me to lead the way. A small piece of me wished he would show, but it was my task since he didn't know where to go. Plus, I was the boss. Was it too late to sell the company?

The break room door slowly creaked open to an eerily silent room. I motioned with a head nod toward the third aisle of cubicles where I saw the computer on when I first came in earlier.

As we grew closer down the aisle, Bob pointed to the desk. Sitting on the file cabinet within the cubicle stood the base of the vine. A bright blue light glowed from within the terra-cotta planter.

"What are you doing, Jessie?" the voices called out from all around us.

"You look thirsty. I thought I would give you some water," I called back.

"Water... yes. We like water. So thirsty."

Bob held me back, shaking his head. It was too easy, and we both knew it.

Vines dropped down from the ceiling, encasing Bob and his axe.

"Bob!" I called out.

"Do it!" he called within a crushing scream.

I quickly unscrewed the cap, finding the foil still covering the top of the bottle. My luck, I'd end up with the new bottle of bleach. My thumb danced around the foil top, unable to penetrate it. Then, scissors on the desk caught my eye. I grabbed the scissors, plunging them into the top of the bleach bottle.

Suddenly, my hand flew into the air, and the scissors, along with my hand, flew deep into my chest. I didn't move... couldn't move. All I could focus on was the cold metal stinging my skin and how hard it was to breathe.

"JESSIE!" Bob coughed out as the vine slowly squeezed the life from his body.

My shaking arm reached out, pouring the bleach into the terracotta planter as my body grew weaker. Finally, I fell to the floor, watching as Bob's body dropped from the ceiling.

Then... It darkened.

POSTMORTEM

I woke three days later in the hospital to the sight of several large flower displays and "Get Well Soon" balloons. To my surprise, Margo was sitting beside my bed.

"Hey, Jessie. How are you feeling?" she asked.

I felt to my chest, feeling a large bandage. "What... happened?" I shot up, instantly remembering. "Bob?"

Margo rested her hand on my shoulder to calm me. "He's fine. Paramedics arrived on the scene just in time and managed to revive him. I called the police when Bob left to find you." She paused, hesitating to continue. "That little plant of Mike's killed twenty-three people in our office and some of their families. Police also found Mike's body. His plant apparently suffocated him in his sleep. There's a good chance he never knew what he created."

"What... what about the plants?" I croaked.

Margo shook her head. I could tell she was frowning behind her pink mask. "The government took over. I guess they destroyed all of the plants. I'm sure someone will be in shortly to speak to you about what happened. Until then," she stood, patting my shoulder, "get some rest."

"Margo, do me a favor?" I called out before she could leave. She turned back to me. "Have someone get rid of all these plants."

EPILOGUE

After getting discharged from the hospital, I was questioned why was there no CCTV footage by the FBI. I was baffled, all my statements had no evidence and when I said about the plants, FBI wasn't convinced, I returned to office for the search any small piece of proof to show what happened and that's when **All hell broke loose**!!

TO BE CONTINUED...

ACKNOWLEDGEMENT

I would like to acknowledge my wife, parents, mentors, well wishers who believed in my writing ability and supported me in all my endeavours, without you people, I am just a rock. Thank you from my bottom of my heart.

ABOUT THE AUTHOR

Dhineshsunder Ganapathi

A Techie, Chess player, blogger and a digital nomad, Dhinesh is a perfect baggage of Unorthodox Introvert who is interested in exploring new stuffs, and currently in the pursuit of telling stories to the masses